STRIKES AGAIN

Lincoln Peirce

BiG NATE STRIKES AGAIN

SCHOLASTIC INC.

ISBN 978-0-545-83206-9

12 11 10 9 8 7 6 5 4 3 2 1   15 16 17 18 19 20/0

Printed in the U.S.A.   23

First Scholastic printing, January 2015

Typography by Sasha Illingworth

To Elias, from your friend and admirer

CHAPTER 1

"That's the ugliest baby I've ever seen."

GUESS THAT BABY!

Teddy and I are standing in the entrance hall of our school, P.S. 38, in front of a bulletin board covered with a gajillion baby pictures. I've never seen so much pink and blue in my life.

"Which one?" I chuckle, peering over his shoulder for a closer look.

What?? Hey, WAIT a minute! . . .

"It IS??" Teddy says. He's trying to act all shocked, but I can tell by the look on his face he knew it was my picture all along.

"Yup. That's Nate, all right," says Francis, walking up behind us.

Francis and Teddy are my two best friends—which might surprise you, considering how they're ragging on me about this baby picture. But that's just the way the three of us operate. They both know it's only a matter of time before I find something to bust THEIR chops about. It all evens out in the end.

"Well, what about YOU, Francis?" I say, quickly locating his photo on the board.

Francis shrugs. "Hey, ALL babies are kind of chunky," he says. "Where do you think the phrase 'baby fat' comes from?"

"From your picture, obviously," snorts Teddy.

He waves at all the photos on the board.

Before Francis and I give Teddy a tag-team noogie for being so obnoxious, maybe I should explain what's up with all these baby pictures.

This is Mrs. Shipulski's bulletin board. She's the school secretary, and she's in charge of what goes on it. Usually it's covered with lame posters, like:

 or . . .

But last week Mrs. Shipulski decided to try some-thing different. Here's what happened:

Actually, that last part didn't really happen. I just wanted to jazz up the story.

Anyway, that's how the P.S. 38 Guess That Baby game got started. Mrs. Shipulski asked every single kid in the sixth grade to put a picture on this board.

"Some of these are so easy to guess," Francis says.

"And there's Chester," Teddy says, pointing at another one.

I'm not really listening to Teddy and Francis. I'm scanning the board from left to right, searching for one . . . specific . . . picture.

There! Sandwiched between a couple of kids having really bad hair days—that's her!

AH-HA!

"Who'd you find?" Francis asks.

"Take a look!" I say.

Francis and Teddy step up to examine the picture more closely. They look confused. As usual.

"I give up," Teddy says finally. "Who is it?"

"Isn't it OBVIOUS?" I say.

Jenny's the most awesome girl in the whole sixth grade, and someday she and I are going to make a great couple. (Unfortunately, she's going out with Artur at the moment, which is kind of a drag. But that'll change.) The point is, I'm a Jenny expert.

"I recognized her right away," I go on. "She's the best-looking baby here. By FAR!"

Ugh. Look who just oozed in. Gina. How is this any of HER business?

"Of COURSE I'm sure," I snap at Gina. "I'm POSITIVE!"

"Oh, really?" says Gina with an obnoxious little smirk. "Well, maybe you don't know her as well as you THINK you do!"

She marches over to the board . . .

. . . and starts pulling the picture off.

"Hey, you can't do that!" I shout. "That's not yours!"

Gina walks toward me. "Well, if it's not mine," she asks . . .

She holds it up close to my face. There, written on the back, I see:

Gina Hemphill-Toms   age 14 months

I blink hard and look again, hoping that maybe I read it wrong. But there's no mistake. This isn't a picture of Jenny. It's Gina. I feel like I just got clubbed on the forehead with a Louisville Slugger.

With a nasty grin, Gina throws my own words back at me:

Teddy and Francis explode with laughter. So do some other kids who've started to crowd around. And there's nothing I can do about it. This is like one of those bad dreams where everyone else has clothes on and you're in your underwear.

Gina puts the picture back, then walks away, waving at everybody like a stinkin' prom queen.

I just might puke. Here I am, standing in front of half the school, looking like a visitor from Planet Moron. But I can deal with that. I've done it before. What makes this the absolute pits is knowing that it was Gina who got the best of me.

Gina's one of my least favorite people. No, more than that. She's one of my least favorite ANYTHINGS. Check out my list:

THINGS I CAN'T STAND!

by: 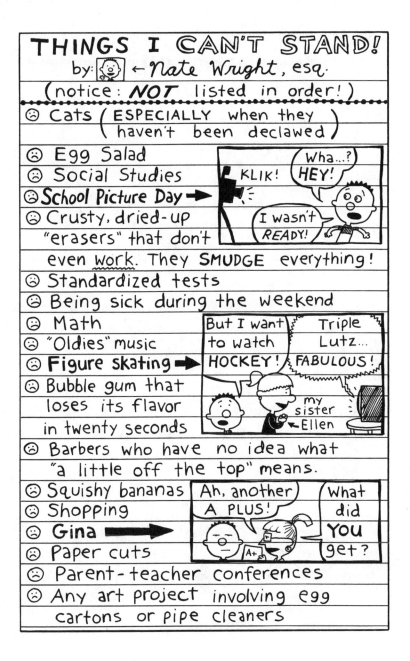 ← *Nate Wright*, esq.

(notice: **NOT** listed in order!)

- ☹ Cats (ESPECIALLY when they haven't been declawed)
- ☹ Egg Salad
- ☹ Social Studies
- ☹ *School Picture Day* ➡
- ☹ Crusty, dried-up "erasers" that don't even work. They **SMUDGE** everything!

> KLIK!
> Wha...?
> HEY!
> I wasn't READY!

- ☹ Standardized tests
- ☹ Being sick during the weekend
- ☹ Math
- ☹ "Oldies" music
- ☹ **Figure skating** ➡
- ☹ Bubble gum that loses its flavor in twenty seconds

> But I want to watch HOCKEY!
> Triple Lutz... FABULOUS!
> my sister ← Ellen

- ☹ Barbers who have no idea what "a little off the top" means.
- ☹ Squishy bananas
- ☹ Shopping
- ☹ **Gina** ➡
- ☹ Paper cuts

> Ah, another A PLUS!
> What did YOU get?
> A+

- ☹ Parent-teacher conferences
- ☹ Any art project involving egg cartons or pipe cleaners

That makes it pretty clear, right? When you're comparing someone to egg salad and figure skating, that's about as low as it gets.

"Oh, come on," says Francis. "You don't HATE her."

"Yes, I do," I growl.

"Well, just remember what they say," Teddy says with a smile. "It's a fine line between hate and . . ."

Francis snickers. "You two will make a LOVELY couple," he says when he finally pulls himself together.

I'm about to knock their heads together, Three Stooges style . . .

. . . when the bell rings for homeroom.

I'm no fan of homeroom—hey, it's ten minutes of sharing oxygen with Mrs. Godfrey—but I'm all for anything that'll shut up Francis and Teddy. In I go.

New seat assignments? Fine. Whatever. I don't really care where I sit. I just want class to start so I can put all this Gina stuff . . .

2

You're probably wondering: What's up with Nate
drinking all the Gina Hater-ade? Is she really that
bad?

Uh, that would be a yes. With a capital Y.

It's tough to say what it is about Gina that bugs me the most. There's so much to choose from. But here's a big one: She's always talking about how GREAT she is.

Francis says that maybe Gina just ACTS like she's better than everybody else because deep down she doesn't really like herself. He might have a point. If I were Gina, I wouldn't like myself either. But Gina's taking up way too much space in my brain this morning. I really need to start thinking about something else.

Like the fact that class started five seconds ago, and Mrs. Godfrey's already yelling.

And now she's pulling out her blue folder. Oh, no.

Mrs. Godfrey color codes everything. Her yellow folder is for attendance sheets. The green one is for homework assignments. The red one's filled with in-class work sheets. And the blue one?

"Special projects." And I don't mean special in a good way. In middle school, "special" is like a dirty word.

The last time we did a special project, Mrs. Godfrey only gave me a C plus on my Louisiana report because she said I wrote too much stuff about pelicans. HELLO!? The pelican happens to be the state bird of Louisiana! That was vital info!

And the time before that, she gave me a lousy grade on my replica of the Colosseum because

I built it out of Legos. Well, what did she EXPECT me to do? Go to the nearest quarry and dig up some marble?

"I'm going to tell you about a new special project, class," Mrs. Godfrey announces. She's smiling, which is never a good sign. Plus, whenever she shows her teeth it reminds me of a shark attack on Animal Planet.

Ugh. A research paper. That's a biggie. Those things take weeks to do. And they usually count a ton toward your semester grade.

"AND . . . ," she continues . . .

YES!! Finally, some good news!

I look over at Teddy and Francis. I can tell we're all thinking the same thing. We jump up from our chairs and head straight for the front of the room.

She looks like she just smelled something foul. "I don't THINK so," she says.

SPECIAL PROJECT FACT:
The only time she let the three of us work together, we built a model of Mount Vesuvius and accidentally splattered her with fake lava.

WHOOPS.

"First of all, you will be working in PAIRS, not groups of three," she says, sounding like she expected us to know that already. "And SECOND of all . . . I'll be matching students RANDOMLY."

She pulls out a cookie jar from her bottom drawer. Not that there are any cookies in it, of course. She probably ate them all. She sure didn't offer US any.

"I'll select two names at a time," Mrs. Godfrey explains. "The classmate you're paired with will be your partner for this project."

Wow. This is like one of those lottery drawings on TV, where a babe picks numbered Ping-Pong balls out of a giant fish tank. Except Mrs. Godfrey's not using Ping-Pong balls. And she's not a babe.

The class starts buzzing. We all understand the stakes.

You could end up with someone great, or you could get stuck with a total dud.

The best partners are pretty obvious: Francis or Teddy would be fantastic. Getting paired with Jenny would be beyond awesome. And of course whoever gets paired up with ME is hitting a major jackpot.

But in every class, there are always a few kids like this:

The suspense is killing everybody. What's the holdup here? Mrs. Godfrey's just standing by her desk, staring at us.

 Oh. I get it. She's doing that thing teachers always do, when they get all quiet and wait for the class to figure out that it's time to shut up.

Finally she reaches into the jar and picks out the first two slips. "Kendra . . . ," she reads aloud, ". . . and Matthew."

I shoot a quick look at Kendra and Matthew. They don't exactly look thrilled, but I'm pretty sure they both realize one thing:

Mrs. Godfrey continues . . .

"Brian and Kelly . . . Molly and Allison . . . Jenny and Artur . . . Kim and Nick . . . Cindy and Steven . . ."

Wait, hold it. Rewind. Did I hear that right?

Great. Those two are practically joined at the hip as it is. Now they'll be spending even MORE time together. This is an OUTRAGE!

Oh, come ON! First Jenny and Artur, and now Teddy and Francis get to work together? Look at them over there. They're acting like they just won a trip to Disney World.

But what about ME? I scan the classroom and do some quick calculating. There are only a few names Mrs. Godfrey hasn't chosen.

My stomach does a swan dive down to my shoes. Gina hasn't been paired with anybody yet.

Oh, please, no. PLEASE don't let me get stuck with Gina. ANYONE but her.

Mrs. Godfrey reaches into the jar again.

What a RELIEF!! I'm fine with being Megan's partner. MORE than fine. Megan's pretty cool. She's nice, she's smart . . .

She's not here. Megan? Anybody seen Megan?

"Oh, wait," says Mrs. Godfrey. "I just remembered Megan's having her tonsils removed this week. She'll be absent for a while."

"B-but I don't mind waiting until Megan gets back," I stammer. "I'll just—"

"QUIET, Nate," Mrs. Godfrey barks. Before I can get another word out, she's got her hand back in the cookie jar. "You'll be working with . . ."

"Is there a PROBLEM, you two?" Mrs. Godfrey asks in a tone that makes it clear there'd better not be.

Typical Gina. She says exactly what the teacher wants to hear. But I can't pretend everything's fine and dandy when it isn't. Mrs. Godfrey's eyes look like they're about to burn a hole in my head. But she asked if there's a problem, and I'm going to give her an answer.

"Really?" she answers, sounding surprised. "Well, I can't imagine WHY!"

A few kids snicker. Mrs. Godfrey turns and starts writing on the blackboard. That's her way of telling me this conversation is over. There's no way out. I'm officially partners with Gina.

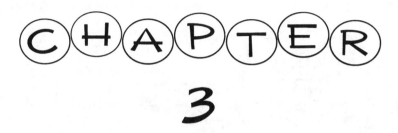

CHAPTER 3

"I'm so mad at Megan's tonsils," I grumble as Francis, Teddy, and I stop by our lockers.

"Right," says Francis. "I'm sure that was all part of Megan's master plan."

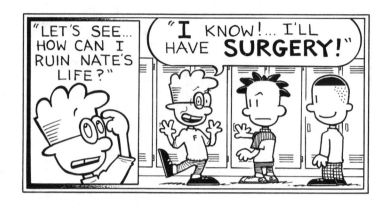

"Okay, okay," I say. "You don't have to make it sound so stupid."

"Well, Mrs. Godfrey won't let you dump Gina," Francis points out, "so you might as well make the best of it."

"Easy for YOU to say," I shoot back. "YOU'RE not the one stuck with her!"

Groan. Gina and her precious academic record. I've only heard this about a thousand times.

"You know what, Gina? I could do as well as you if I really wanted to," I tell her.

"Then why DON'T you?"

"Because," I answer, "there's more to life than good grades!"

"Listen, Einstein," Gina snarls. "When you're working with ME . . ."

"Our paper topic is Benjamin Franklin," she says slowly. "Think you can remember that?"

I don't answer. Actually, I CAN'T answer, what with Gina strangling me and all. Finally she lets me go and stalks off toward—shocker!—the library. Her home away from home.

"Mrs. Godfrey was right," Teddy teases.

I'm about to hip check him into the water fountain when . . .

"Guys!" I say excitedly. "It's TUESDAY!"

Pause.

"Congratulations," says Francis. "Did you figure that out all by yourself?"

That perks them up. We head for the gym as fast as we can. We don't run, because if you get caught running in the hallways, you get detention.

So we just walk super-fast, even though it makes you look like you need to go to the bathroom really, really bad.

Great timing. Coach is putting up the list just as we're racewalking around the corner.

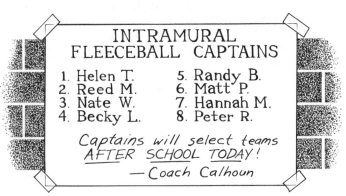

INTRAMURAL
FLEECEBALL CAPTAINS

1. Helen T.   5. Randy B.
2. Reed M.   6. Matt P.
3. Nate W.   7. Hannah M.
4. Becky L.   8. Peter R.

Captains will select teams
AFTER SCHOOL TODAY!
— Coach Calhoun

There are two kinds of sports at P.S. 38: the official ones you play against other schools, like soccer and basketball and lacrosse; and the UNofficial ones that you play between seasons. All the teachers call them intramurals, but the kids call them SPOFFs:

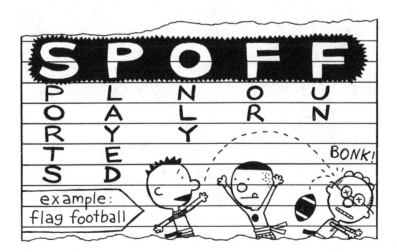

I've got to be honest: They're not played ONLY for fun. You're playing against kids you've known your whole life, so it can get pretty intense. It's more than sports. It's bragging rights.

And there's a trophy.

It's the sorriest-looking thing you've ever seen. But SPOFFs are such a big deal, a long time ago somebody decided there had to be a trophy. So they wrapped some aluminum foil around an empty Dr Pepper can and called it the Spoffy, the most idiotic name for a trophy of all time.

I want to win that stupid thing so bad. I've just got to.

My SPOFF career has been a disaster so far. It's not my fault. I just keep ending up on lame teams.

And the one time I was actually on a half-decent team?

Dodgeball: Good news: We made it to the championship game. Bad news: So did the other team.

POW!

←(Chester)

Speed: 1,000,000,000 miles per hour

So obviously I've never won the Spoffy. But here's why this is my big chance. First, I'm a captain. That means I get to pick my own team! It's not random, like that cookie jar thing in social studies.

EL CAPITÁN

Second, I'm really good at fleeceball. But if you don't have fleeceball at your school, you probably have no idea what I'm talking about.

Fleeceball is indoor baseball. Most of the rules are the same, except instead of a baseball bat, you use a broom handle. The ball's puffy, so it doesn't hurt if it hits you. Last year Chad got drilled right in the face, and he was totally fine.

And one more thing: It's not a good idea to slide when you're running the bases.

"You're gonna pick me for your team, right, Nate?" asks Teddy.

"Of COURSE I am, as long as another captain doesn't pick you first," I say.

Randy's a bully. He walks around acting like he owns the school, and he's always got a posse of five or six guys trailing after him like a bunch of pilot fish. And I don't even think THEY like him. They just PRETEND to like him because they're afraid of him.

"Step aside, scrubs," he barks at us. Then he checks the list. He does a little fist pump when he sees his name.

Then he looks at it again and turns toward me.

"Coach made YOU a captain?" he says.

Is Randy trying to trash-talk me? Fine. Bring it on.

"I AM good at sports," I tell him. "But it takes more than that to be a captain."

"Like what?" he sneers.

"I'll show you," I say.

I lead Randy and his crew down the hallway. I sneak a couple of looks over my shoulder to make sure they're still with me. So far, so good.

We stop.

"What's this all about?" Randy demands.

"I told you I was going to show you an important part of being a captain," I say, turning toward my locker. "Here it is."

Randy tries to say something, but he can't. He's too busy getting crushed by the avalanche of garbage that just exploded out of my locker. I guess being a slob has its advantages.

He'll probably kill me later. And maybe his fleece-ball team will totally destroy mine. But right now, I really don't care. I went up against the biggest jerk in school, and I won.

Score!

CHAPTER 4

News travels fast in middle school. It took about five seconds for the whole sixth grade to hear how I punked Randy.

Mr. Big Shot isn't used to getting laughed at. So he's probably got one thing on his mind:

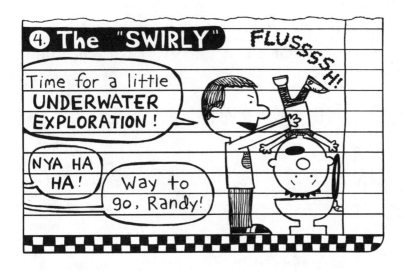

He's been looking for me all day. But he'll never find me here. I'm in the library.

I wasn't PLANNING to be in the library. Five minutes ago I was in science, my last class of the day. But then things got a little out of hand. That seems to happen to me a lot.

It started out okay. Mr. Galvin said we were doing an experiment about energy. That was funny, because Mr. Galvin and energy don't exactly go together.

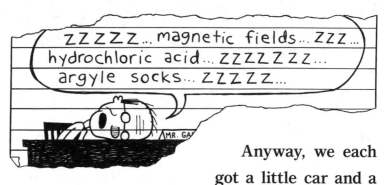

Anyway, we each got a little car and a board to use as a ramp. We were supposed to keep changing the angle of the ramp, and measure how far the car rolled each time.

Guess what? The steeper the ramp, the farther the car went. Duh. What's next, doing an experiment to prove water is wet?

The whole thing was a day trip to Camp Boredom. And then I got the idea to liven things up by customizing my car.

I turned it into the BATMOBILE! Pretty cool, right? So then I figured: Why stop there?

Yeah, it was probably a little goofy, but I was getting laughs. AND it was making science FUN for a change. Until . . .

Ever notice that teachers always ask what you're doing when anybody with half a brain could figure it out? I didn't know what Mr. Galvin wanted me to say, so I decided to go with Old Reliable:

NNNNNNNNNNN
NNNNNNNNNNNN
NNNNNNOTHING.

I guess Mr. Galvin's not a big Batman fan. His jaw muscles started to twitch, which always means trouble. I expected him to launch into one of those screaming fits where his voice gets all weird and shaky. But he just gave one of those "I'm-so-disappointed-in-you" sighs and said:

IF YOU'RE NOT GOING TO **APPLY** YOURSELF DURING **CLASS**...

...WHY DON'T YOU SPEND THE REST OF THE PERIOD IN THE **LIBRARY**?

The library? I didn't see THAT one coming, but, hey, fine by me. I cleaned things up, headed for the door . . .

. . . and then the other shoe dropped.

Shoot. It's bad enough getting yelled at during school hours. But getting chewed out on my OWN time?

Still, it's better than sitting in science watching Mr. Galvin's arteries harden. The library's my favorite hangout spot in school. It's perfect for table football. There are hardly ever any teachers here. And best of all . . .

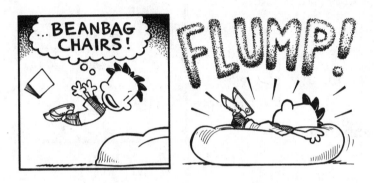

I snuggle deep into the chair. Ahhhh, this is nice. I'll just relax here for a while and . . .

Oop. It's Hickey. Mrs. Hickson, I mean. She's the head librarian, and she's not really into "hanging out." I'm pretty sure the bean-bag chairs weren't her idea. If you're in her library, she wants to see you DOING something.

"Well, then," she answers, "wouldn't a BOOK come in handy?"

Librarians. Aren't they hilarious?

Great. So much for my date with the beanbag chair. Instead I'm stuck reading about some guy who's been worm food for a couple of centuries.

Except . . . you know what?

This Ben Franklin dude was actually pretty cool!

Before now, all I knew about Ben Franklin was that a) he was kind of chubby, and b) his picture is on the hundred-dollar bill. But it turns out that he did all sorts of amazing stuff back in Colonial times. Basically, the man was a genius. Like me.

I open my binder and start taking notes.

"Nate," calls Mrs. Hickson from the front desk. "The bell rang."

It did? Wow, I got so wrapped up in my work that I didn't hear a thing.

I hurry toward the science room, hoping Mr. Galvin isn't there. Maybe he went home. Maybe he forgot about me.

No such luck.

Whoa, hold on. Did he just call me a show-off? That is SO bogus. I wasn't showing off, I was just trying to make science a little more interesting. Or did

Mr. Galvin miss the fact that his little car and ramp experiment was a total yawnathon?

"School is serious business, Nate," he continues. "It's not fun and games."

Fun and games.

Oh, NO!!!

I'm supposed to be in the GYM right now! I have to pick players for my fleeceball team!!

I break into a sweat. Mr. Galvin's still flapping his gums, but I can't just stand here and wait for him to shut up.

Silence. Okay, mission accomplished. He stopped talking. But did I just make things worse?

"All right then, Nate," he says finally. "I accept your apology."

I'm out the door and on my way to the gym at about warp 10. Forget that whole "no running in the hallways" rule. This is an emergency!

"I'm afraid you're too late, Nate," Coach tells me. "The captains' meeting is over."

"Over?" I say, my heart sinking. I feel my chance to win the Spoffy slipping away. "But—"

Coach reads my mind. "Don't worry, Nate," he says with a smile. "You're still a captain. And you've got yourself a team."

For a second, I feel a little twinge of disappointment. I was really looking forward to picking the team myself. But then I start reading the roster Coach gave me.

Francis and Teddy are on my team! YES!! And there are a lot of other good players here, too!

"Wow, this team could be a POWERHOUSE!" I exclaim. "Thanks, Coach!"

Coach looks confused for a second. He glances over my shoulder.

I slide my thumb to the side. There, at the bottom of the list, is the tenth name. No! NO!!

I almost gag. Is this some kind of sick JOKE? What's Gina doing signing up for fleeceball? She doesn't even LIKE sports. She's going to ruin everything!

Whoa. Wait a sec. My team. MY team.

I'M the captain. I'M in charge. The other players have to do what I say. Including Gina.

Maybe this won't be so bad after all. Maybe, for once, I've got Gina right where I want her.

CHAPTER 5

"What's our team called?" Francis asks as the three of us walk home.

"Nothing," I say.

I ignore them. "I didn't have a name ready when I talked to Coach," I explain. "So he gave me until homeroom tomorrow to come up with one."

"Well, make sure it's a GOOD one," Teddy says. "There's nothing worse than being on a team with a bad name."

Yeah, that was pretty embarrassing.

"Still, we DID have a pretty catchy slogan," Francis reminds us.

We reach my house. "Well, one season as a Hot Dog was enough," I say. "I definitely won't be giving us some stupid FOOD name."

"So we're not going to be Nate's Noodles?" Teddy asks.

"How about you clowns let an EXPERT handle this? By tomorrow I'll have the perfect team name."

"Gina's Gerbils!" Teddy calls.

"Hi, Nate," says Dad from the kitchen. "How was school?"

"Not bad," I say, my stomach rumbling. All that talk about hot dogs and tacos made me hungry.

"Sure," says Dad. "Whatever you can find."

Whatever I can find? Good one, Dad. See, our house isn't like other houses. Welcome to . . .

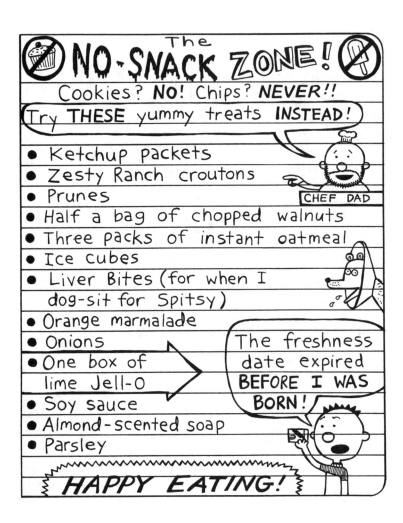

This is pathetic. Would it kill Dad to keep a few bags of Cheez Doodles lying around? I'm about to start gnawing on a table leg when . . .

Oop. That's my cue to go up to my room. I don't need to listen to Ellen blabbing away about all the boys who never notice her or what kind of lip gloss she's going to wear tomorrow.

"Who is it?" I ask.

"How should I know?" answers Ellen. She's obviously devastated that the call isn't for her.

A girl??? That hardly ever happens. The last time a girl called me, it was Annette Bingham selling Girl Scout cookies. I'm trying to figure out who it might be when a thought hits me:

How awesome would THAT be? I try to stay calm as I reach for the phone. Very cool. Very suave.

Ugh. Letdown City. Gina's voice sounds even more annoying over the phone. If that's possible.

"Have you done any Ben Franklin research yet?" she snaps.

Wait a minute, is she CHECKING UP on me? "As a matter of fact, I HAVE," I say. "Not that it's any of your business."

"Chillax, Gina. I'm not going to screw up your perfect record."

"You'd better not," she barks. "Because any grade below an A plus would mean . . ."

The old low-battery trick. Works every time.

"Who was on the phone?" Dad asks hopefully. Uh, sorry, Dad. The only people who ever call you are telemarketers.

Thanks SO much, Ellen. Now Dad's going to get all parental on me.

"A GIRL!" he says, raising his eyebrows. "Really?"

"It wasn't a girl," I mutter. "It was Gina."

Okay, this is officially grossing me out. "NO!" I yell, almost gagging. "Gina's my ARCHENEMY!"

"Ooh!" Ellen chimes in. "Mrs. Godfrey?"

Whoops. Big mistake. I should never mention Mrs. Godfrey around Ellen, because . . .

See? The floodgates have opened. And now she's running up to her room and coming back with . . .

That's a big difference between Ellen and me. She saves her report cards. I burn mine.

Ellen sounds giddy. "Want to hear some of the comments Mrs. Godfrey gave me back then?"

"Ahem!" she begins.

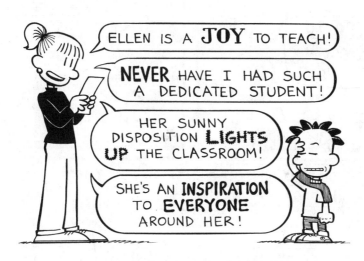

This is disgusting. I stomp up to my room. If I wanted to hear someone brag about her grades, I would have stayed on the phone with Gina.

Besides, I already knew that Mrs. Godfrey is the world's number one Ellen fan. She made that clear the night of the P.S. 38 Open House.

Don't get me wrong. It's not that I really WANT Mrs. Godfrey to like me. The kids she likes are all a bunch of dweebs. But sixth grade would be a lot easier for me . . .

Okay, enough about Ellen. Thanks to her little Me-Fest—and Gina's phone call—I haven't had time to focus on what's REALLY important:

I need a name that stands out. A lot of kids name their SPOFF teams after their favorite pro team. What's fun about THAT? Where's the imagination? I want to come up with something ORIGINAL.

I grab a pencil. Time to start brainstorming.

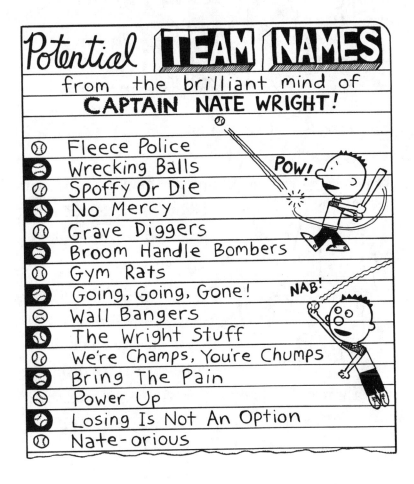

Potential TEAM NAMES

from the brilliant mind of **CAPTAIN NATE WRIGHT!**

1. Fleece Police
2. Wrecking Balls
3. Spoffy Or Die
4. No Mercy
5. Grave Diggers
6. Broom Handle Bombers
7. Gym Rats
8. Going, Going, Gone!
9. Wall Bangers
10. The Wright Stuff
11. We're Champs, You're Chumps
12. Bring The Pain
13. Power Up
14. Losing Is Not An Option
15. Nate-orious

Hmm. These are good, but none of 'em are knocking my socks off.

Holy cow! Is that SPITSY?

Spitsy belongs to our neighbor Mr. Eustis, and compared to other dogs, he's sort of lame. He wears a ridiculous purple sweater and a halo collar that makes him look like a walking satellite dish. He has a knack for jumping on you right after he's been rolling around in something dead. And one time, he infested my backpack with fleas.

But he's never LOUD. I run to the window to see what's got him so freaked out. Looks like Spitsy's barking at . . .

. . . nothing.

Maybe something WAS there a second ago. Maybe he saw a cat, or maybe a squirrel ran by. I can't see anything now. But Spitsy's still going completely psycho.

Hey! That's IT!

Remember how I said I wanted my team to stand out? Well, this is just the name to do it. It's perfect. I can't wait to tell the guys.

They'll be crazy about it.

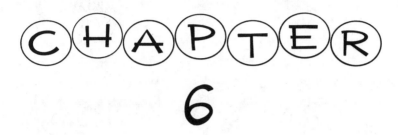

CHAPTER 6

I was right. When I tell Francis and Teddy that we're going to be the Psycho Dogs, they're totally into it. So the day's off to a great start.

Oop. That didn't last long.

Chad's right. As we get closer to the school yard, I can see Randy and his little gang of sidekicks hanging out by the tetherball pole. You don't have to be Einstein to figure out his plan.

But no need to panic. I've got the school yard safety policy on my side.

I don't think they even HAD a safety policy until last year. But then came the Eric Fleury Incident.

Eric's completely obsessed with martial arts stuff. He'll be doing something normal, like standing in the lunch line. And then, for no reason, he'll break into a bunch of kung fu moves. Weird.

One day during recess, Eric and Danny DelFino were play fighting in the school yard, doing kick-boxing and karate and stuff. It was sort of a dork fest, but I have to admit: It looked pretty real.

I guess it looked a little TOO real. Principal Nichols had no clue they were just messing around. He started running toward them. And he almost NEVER runs, not even in the kids versus teachers basketball game.

When they saw him charging at them like a runaway hippo, it must have messed up their super kung fu concentration. They both sort of fell down.

Eric landed funny. You could hear the snap all the way over by the parking lot. He broke his arm.

Of course after that the school went totally overboard. They outlawed play fighting and just about anything else that's fun. Which makes for some pretty boring recesses.

Official **P.S. 38** List of

APPROVED SCHOOL YARD ACTIVITIES!

- Standing quietly
- Sitting quietly
- Doing homework →
- Chatting with others in an appropriate, nonthreatening way
- Listening to teachers tell stories about their lives →
- Yoga
- Poetry
- Yoga and poetry at the same time →
- Picking up trash and gently disposing of it (NO THROWING!!)
- Taking a nap
- Group sing-along →

What FUN!

USELESS FACTS

...and then I put butter on my corn muffin...

Roses are red...
I'll pose on my head!

Hey, gang! I brought my oboe!
CHAD →

But you know what? Right now I'm FINE with the safety policy, because it's going to keep Randy off my back. If he tries anything that even LOOKS like we're fighting, the playground patrol will be all over him. So I'm not worried.

Until I see who's on duty.

Coach John's old-school. I'm pretty sure he doesn't care much about the safety policy. He's always telling us we need a little LESS safety.

If he sees Randy mopping the asphalt with my face, he'll probably just let it happen. He'll say it's good character building.

So I can't count on Coach John to bail me out. And I bet Randy knows it, too. As we walk onto the school yard, he and his posse don't even try to hide the fact they're about to ambush me. I've got a feeling I'm about to replace Eric Fleury as the poster child for school-yard injuries. I can hear it now: Remember the Nate Wright Incident?

Then I get a brilliant idea.

I've got a head start on Randy, but not a big one. And this backpack is slowing me down. I can feel him gaining on me as I motor across the school yard and into the building.

Principal Nichols! Looks like he forgot to take his happy pill this morning.

Recreation? Excuse me, I was running for my LIFE! But I can't say that with Randy standing only two feet away.

Principal Nichols isn't buying it.

I nod, and so does Randy. I guess he wants to stick close to me, what with him wanting to kill me and all.

"Well, then, you BOTH must know the answer to this question . . . "

What was the name of the popular book that Ben Franklin published every year from 1732 to 1758?

"'Poor Richard's Almanack,'" I say immediately.

The Big Guy looks kind of surprised. Maybe even impressed. "Very well, Nate," he says. "You may go to the computer lab."

Whew. That was close. Randy shuffles away, looking even MORE like he wants to kill me. I scoot into the lab before Principal Nichols can slap any more Ben Franklin questions on me.

Speaking of Ben, I wonder if he ever had to deal with jerks like Randy?

There's the bell. I head for homeroom, making sure to avoid Randy. Once classes start, I can sort of relax. He's not in any of my sections.

It's a pretty typical morning. Mrs. Godfrey screams at me a couple of times in social studies. Ms. Clarke gives us some new vocab words in English. (Hey, how about "extremely" and "boring"?) And in art, Mr. Rosa lets us make clay sculptures.

"A WALRUS??" I say. "It's a PSYCHO DOG, you moron!"

"Uh-oh, what?" I ask, still a little peeved.

"Did you remember to tell Coach our team name this morning?" Francis asks.

Coach wanted that name by homeroom! I was so worried about getting away from Randy, I totally forgot!

How stupid can I get? I hope Coach wasn't too mad when I didn't show up.

Finally the bell rings. Thirty seconds later, I'm at his office door.

"Sorry I didn't give you the name of my fleeceball team this morning," I stammer. "I was—"

Coach interrupts me with a friendly smile. "No problem, Nate," he says.

Wait a minute. How'd THAT happen? "You . . . you did?" I ask.

"Right on time . . . ," he says.

Did he say . . . GINA?? The room starts spinning. I open my mouth to speak, but nothing comes out.

"I'm proud of you for letting her pick the name, Nate," Coach continues.

"Wait!" I say as he walks out. "What did Gina . . . ?"

"I printed up the schedule. There are copies on my file cabinet," he calls back to me.

I'm afraid to look.

It's worse than I thought. Worse than ANYBODY could have thought. Gina just turned my fleece-ball team into a total joke. Thanks to her, I'm now the captain of a bunch of . . .

7

I don't care what the schedule says. I'm still going to call us the Psycho Dogs.

But nobody else is.

Great. Coach already posted the schedule. Half the school's seen it by now, and the other half's checking it out on the way into the lunchroom. What a disaster.

Oh, how I hate her. I don't know how she convinced Coach to let her name the team. But I do know she won't get away with it.

Remember my Things I Can't Stand list? Egg salad is on it. So obviously I'm not going to EAT this slop. I have other plans for it.

I do a quick scan of the tables and spot Gina right away. She's sitting near the stage with her pals from the big brain society. Ugh. Look at that stuck-up smile on her face. Okay, Gina, let's see if you're still smiling . . .

I can make it look like an accident. I'll act like I'm on my way to the vending machines, and then my tray will somehow "slip" out of my hands. HA!

Everything stops. The whole lunchroom goes quiet. Until Jenny starts screaming at me.

She's not just mad. She's GODFREY mad. Her eyes look like they could burn a hole in my forehead. She scrapes some of the egg salad out of her hair, and for a second I think she's going to throw it at me. Then Coach shows up.

Mess. That's a pretty good word to describe my day. First Randy goes after me. Then Gina wussifies my fleeceball team. And now Jenny will probably never talk to me again.

Okay, she's still talking to me. So it's not all bad.

I finish cleaning up and find Francis and Teddy.

"This afternoon?"

"Uh, hello? Fleeceball captain?" Francis says. "Our first game's TODAY!"

"And speaking of fleeceball," Teddy says . . .

I tell them the whole story. They're not surprised. They know what a pain Gina is.

YES! We play the scribble game all the time. It's
pretty simple: Somebody makes a scribble . . .

. . . and then you have to turn that scribble into
something.

It's a blast. We're just getting warmed up when . . .

Great. Artur. He's probably ticked off that I dumped egg salad all over Jenny.

"Hallo, guys," he says, smiling. Hm. Guess not. Artur probably doesn't even GET mad. He's too perfect for that.

"Sure!" say Francis and Teddy together. I sort of shrug. Whatever.

Don't get me wrong. I like Artur okay. But it's sort of annoying how nothing ever goes wrong for him. He's never been chased all over the school by Randy. He's never played "drop the lunch tray" with the whole school watching . . . because he's . . .

"Here, Artur," says Teddy, handing him a scribble.

"Better hurry, Artur," Francis says. "The bell rings in two minutes!"

One minute and fifty-nine seconds later:

Holy cow, he drew THAT in two minutes?

"That's AMAZING, Artur!" exclaims Francis.

Yeah, yeah. Let's all stand up and cheer for the amazing Artur. What's he gonna do next, discover a cure for cancer during study hall?

NATE! TODAY AFTER SCHOOL WILL BE **FUN**, YES?

HM?

"I am on Becky's fleeceball team. We are to play-ing yours," he says.

YES! "Oh, really?" I say casually. "Yeah, that'll be fun."

The afternoon's a total snoozeathon—Mr. Galvin busts me for snoring during science—but some-how I make it through. The day's finally over.

Coach goes over a few ground rules (can we move this along, please?) and then the teams split up. "Okay, Psycho Dogs," I call out. "Huddle up!"

"Psycho Dogs?" says Paige.

"Wait, what is THAT thing?" I ask, looking at the lopsided ball of fur in Gina's hand.

I don't know how much more of this I can take. Gina named us after her STUFFED CAT??

Somebody get me a bucket. I'm going to barf.

Coach blows his whistle. "Okay, Killer Bees and Kuddle Kittens," he says . . .

Once the game starts, it doesn't matter WHAT our name is. We PLAY like Psycho Dogs. With Teddy, Francis, and me in the middle of our lineup, we score a bunch of runs right away.

But the other team keeps chipping away at our lead. Not because they're any good, but because they keep hitting the ball to Gina.

She can't catch, she can't throw, she can't hit, she can't run.

Other than that, she's great.

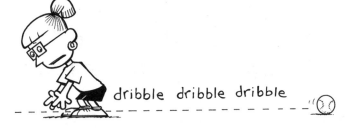

I'd love to sit her on the bench for the whole game. But you can't do that in SPOFFs. Everybody has to play the same amount.

In the fifth inning, she commits four errors. FOUR ERRORS!! I'm getting madder and madder. Does she even CARE? Is she even TRYING??

dribble dribble dribble

"Time out," calls Coach as he walks over to me. Then he lowers his voice.

"Well, maybe Gina feels the same way when she makes an error," he says quietly. "She's not TRYING to fail."

133

I feel my cheeks getting warm. "I know," I say.

"A captain ENCOURAGES his teammates." Coach gives me a smile that makes me feel lousy and good at the same time. The game starts up again.

So what happens? Artur (who else?) gets a lucky bloop hit with the bases loaded. Suddenly we're losing, 9–8. We're down to our last at bats. And Gina's leading off the inning.

She strikes out for the fourth time today. I bite my tongue. Teddy gets a double, so the tying run's on base. But then Francis hits an easy pop-up. Two outs.

And I'm up.

I crush the very first pitch, but it's a foul ball. The second one's right over the plate, and I take a huge hack at it.

That's two strikes. But that's okay. All it takes is one pitch. One swing can tie this game. Or win it.

It's weird: I don't feel nervous at all. I feel totally calm. I wait as the pitcher goes into his windup, watch as the ball leaves his hand. Before the ball's halfway to me, I know I'm going to hit it.

I grip the broom handle as tight as I can . . .

. . . and swing.

CHAPTER 8

"Is there something bothering you, Nate?" asks Dad.

Huh? Oh. Yeah, there's something bothering me. Right here on my plate.

I don't say that, though. When it comes to his cooking, Dad's not a big fan of constructive criticism. Besides, he probably knows it's not really the broccoli that's bumming me out.

"It'll help to talk about it," he says, putting on his best concerned-parent face.

I just shake my head. No offense, Big Guy, but I'm not really in

DAD FACT:
His concerned-parent face is exactly the same as his I-don't-know-how-to-work-the-DVD-player face.

the mood for one of those father-son talks. Not because I don't feel like talking. Because I don't feel like LISTENING.

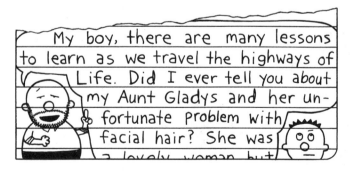

My boy, there are many lessons to learn as we travel the highways of Life. Did I ever tell you about my Aunt Gladys and her unfortunate problem with facial hair? She was a lovely woman but

I hide the rest of my broccoli under my napkin. "May I be excused?"

Dad finally realizes I'm not going to spill my guts. He gives a little shrug and says, "Yes, you may."

 I guess it's nice of him to wonder what's going on. I mean, plenty of parents wouldn't even ASK, right?

But I just don't feel like telling him about that fleeceball game.

I was so sure I was going to hit that stupid ball.

Have you ever been in The Zone? It's not a place. It's a FEELING. It's being 100 percent positive that something is about to happen exactly the way you want it to.

As the ball flew toward me, I was in The Zone. Everything was moving in super slow motion. I was totally focused. I knew what I had to do.

And then . . .

Coach shook his head. "Sorry, Nate," he said. "You can't call interference on your own teammate."

Game over. What a brutal ending. I wanted to take Gina's stuffed cat and rip it into a zillion pieces.

But I didn't. I just gritted my teeth and went through the handshake line.

Losing's bad enough. But when you strike out to end the game—even if it's not your fault!—that's the only thing people remember. There's nothing you can do. You're the goat.

"Nate, your friend Gina is here," Dad says.

Oh, really??? Hey, Dad, thanks for the news flash. Did you ever think of telling me that BEFORE I came downstairs practically butt naked?

I zip down to the basement, my face burning. In half a minute I'm dressed and back in the kitchen. Dad's still Mr. Cheery.

Entertain her? What am I, a clown? How about I just find out what she wants and get RID of her?

"Oh, and Nate," Dad whispers . . .

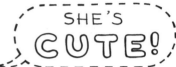

What? CUTE? No, no, no. A puppy is cute. JENNY is cute. Gina is absolutely, positively 100 percent NOT cute.

I'll set him straight later. Right now I have to find something out:

"What do you THINK, brainless?" snarls Gina in her usual charming way. "We're doing a project together. We need to compare notes!"

She pulls out a binder the size of a suitcase and opens it up. It's exactly what you'd expect from Gina. Pages and pages of Ben Franklin research. TYPED. Footnotes. Time lines. I think I even saw a pie chart in there.

"HOLD IT!" she says. "I want to look at YOUR work!"

She smirks. How obnoxious can you get?

"I've done PLENTY of work, Gina," I tell her coldly. "Wait here."

I go up to my room and grab my folder. So she thinks she's the ONLY one who knows anything about Ben Franklin?

I slap my stuff down on the table.

It's pretty impressive, if I do say so myself. There's a little bit of everything here: awesome drawings of major events in Ben's life . . .

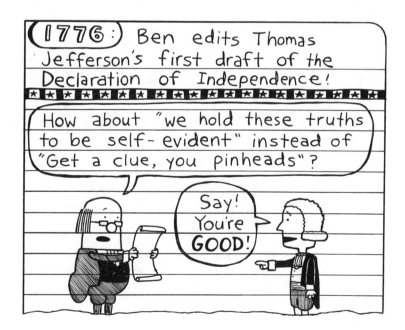

explanations of his amazing inventions . . .

. . . and the REAL story behind some of Ben's famous quotes.

Gina barely looks at it, then gives a little snort. "Is this a JOKE?" she says. "We're not putting CARTOONS in our report!"

"If you stick these dumb drawings in my report, you'll ruin my A plus average!" she whines.

"Oh, really?"

"I don't even want to play on your stupid team!" she shouts.

I yell right back at her.

Gina thinks for a second. "Okay," she says. "I won't . . ."

"YOUR report?" I say. "Mrs. Godfrey told us to work TOGETHER."

"No problem," she says. "I'll do the report, but I'll put both our names on it."

I've got to admit, this is sounding like a pretty good plan. "And you'll quit the fleeceball team?" I ask.

"You can't just quit SPOFFs for no reason," she reminds me.

"Well, you're the brainiac, Gina," I tell her.

"Fine." She nods. "It's a deal."

He sets the tray down and flashes us a sappy smile.
Wait, does he think that . . . ?

"You weren't interrup—" I start to say.

"You two just keep on doing . . . well, whatever it is you're doing." He chuckles.

CHAPTER 9

Poor  Nate's

Price: $1.00

ALMANACK

our motto:

"Read the latest, NATE'S the greatest!"

Welcome to the first edition of P.N.A., inspired by BEN FRANKLIN (the Nate Wright of colonial times)! Looking for up-to-date NEWS, fun *PUZZLES* and COMICS, & Poor Nate's WORDS OF WISDOM? Then *READ ON!!*

◨⊞◣'◩ ◪⊡▨◫ ◪ ◪▨◣◩=◨ ◨◨▨◨!

SOME kids have asked ~~Godzilla~~ Mrs. Godfrey for an extension. **BUT**...

SHARON

...she just smiled and said: **NO EXTENSIONS, NO EXCEPTIONS!**

Hey, **CALM DOWN**, everybody! Remember, Ben Franklin never even **MADE** it to sixth grade... and look how awesome **HE** turned out!

* * * * * * * * * *

POOR NATE PROVERB:

"Why stress out and overwork
When your teacher's such a jerk?"

And now let's see what's going on...

 !

It's time for

CLASSROOM CHATTER!

DID YOU KNOW that you can learn all kinds of private info and juicy gossip by hanging around outside the teachers' lounge? It's **TRUE!** I recently did just that, and HERE's what I overheard:

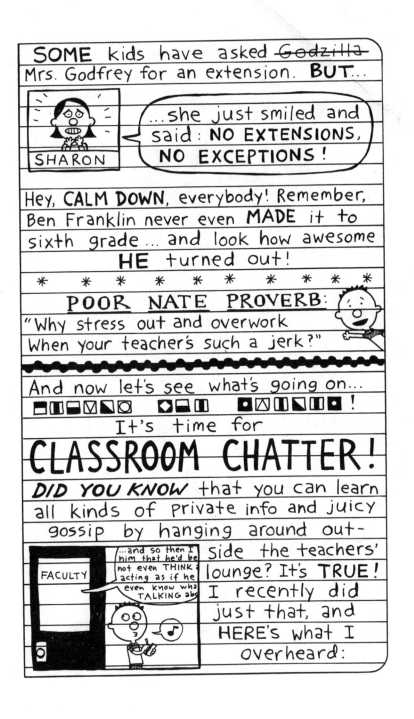

FACULTY
...and so then I
him that he'd be
not even THINK
acting as if he
even know wha
TALKING ab

TAKE HIS ADVICE or PAY THE PRICE!

ETHAN R. TWIG!

Who **IS** this *MYSTERY COLUMNIST*?

DEAR ETHAN: In Math, I sit in front of a kid whose nose whistles when he breathes. I can't hear anything Mr. Staples says! What can I do?? Signed, Perplexed

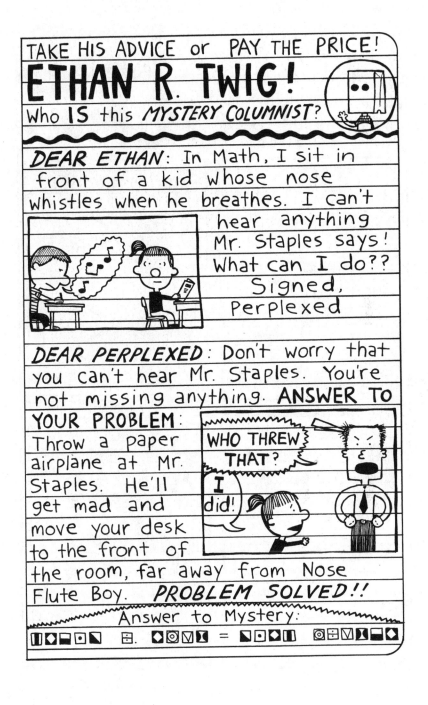

DEAR PERPLEXED: Don't worry that you can't hear Mr. Staples. You're not missing anything. **ANSWER TO YOUR PROBLEM**: Throw a paper airplane at Mr. Staples. He'll get mad and move your desk to the front of the room, far away from Nose Flute Boy. *PROBLEM SOLVED!!*

WHO THREW THAT?

I did!

Answer to Mystery:

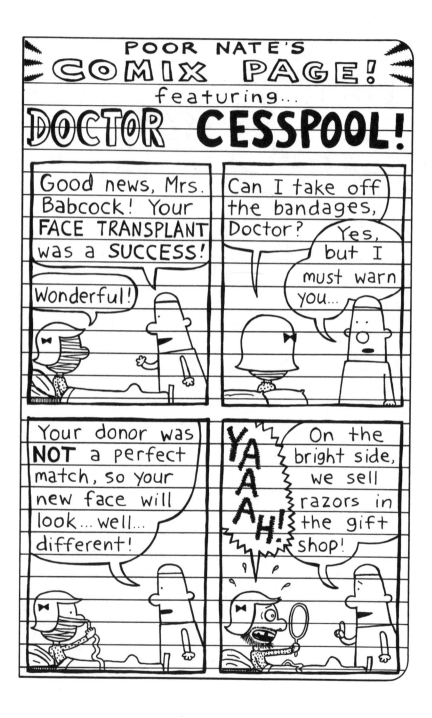

POOR NATE'S 4-SQUARE PUZZLE

Solve the clues...

Then fill in the boxes!

	1.	2.	3.	4.
1.				
2.				
3.				
4.				

ACROSS

1. Piggy _____
2. Not closed
3. He is the **COOLEST!**
4. Mrs. Godfrey's threat: "study or _____!"

DOWN

1. Spitsy chews one.
2. Teddy is such _ ____. (2 words)
3. They hang from hoops.
4. In gym, we do deep ____ bends.

🅇🔲🔳🔲◆🔲🔲◤🕮 :

◆🔳🔲🔲 🔲 🔲🔳🔲 ◉🔻🔲🔲 🔲🔳🔳🔲🔲🔲🔲 🔲🔲🔲 🔳🔲🔲🔳🔲🔲🔲... 🔲🔲🔲🔲🔲🔲◆ 🔲🔲◆🔲🔲!

TODAY'S RIDDLE:

Q. When lightning strikes an orchestra, who gets hit first?

A. The conductor!

PUZZLE SOLUTION:

	1.	2.	3.	4.
1.	B	A	N	K
2.	O	P	E	N
3.	N	A	T	E
4.	E	L	S	E

SPOTLIGHT ON SPOFFS

The fleeceball season got off to a horrible start for the Kuddle Kittens (<u>real</u> name: Psycho Dogs) when they lost to the Killer Bees, 9-8. But led by dynamic team captain *NATE WRIGHT*, the KK's put that game behind them. They have not lost **SINCE!**

↘ *HIGHLIGHTS* of the *SEASON* ↙

Teddy makes an amazing, game-saving grab against the Pumas.

Francis smacks a run-scoring, extra inning double against the Grizzlies.

Nate strikes out TWELVE BATTERS in a win over the Cyclones.

And we **crush** the Chargers in fleeceball... **AND** trash-talking!

Your team didn't **DESERVE** to win! You got **LUCKY!**

If it hadn't been for a couple of che... hi... would... to... you... ys... A... that... wa... so... and YAK... YAK... YAK... YAK YAK YAK... YAK

"Well **DONE** is better than well **SAID.**"

↑ Ben Franklin quote

! !

CURRENT FLEECEBALL STANDINGS

TEAM	WINS-LOSSES
1. Kuddle Kittens	5 – 1
2. Raptors	5 – 1
3. Grizzlies	4 – 3
4. Chargers	4 – 3
5. Pumas	3 – 4
6. Cyclones	3 – 4
7. Killer Bees	3 – 4
8. Road Runners	0 – 7

There's only *ONE GAME LEFT!*

KUDDLE KITTENS VS. **RAPTORS**

Captain: N. Wright

Captain: R. **BUTT**ancourt

"You're asking people to pay you a DOLLAR for this?" asks Francis as he flips through a copy of "Poor Nate's Almanack."

"Yup," I answer proudly.

Francis rolls his eyes.

"I think you should add a horoscope to the next edition," Teddy says, "so people can read their fortunes."

Uh-oh. Principal Nichols. How come he's roaming around the hallways? Is somebody giving away free doughnuts?

"I'm selling an almanac," I tell him. "I'm a writer, a publisher, and a businessman! . . ."

See how I tied it in with the whole social studies thing? Is that smart or what?

"I admire your initiative, Nate," he says.

"But people sell stuff in school all the TIME!" I protest.

The cheerleaders sell t-shirts...	The science club sells candy bars...
BE A BOBCAT BOOSTER!	It's the calcium phosphate that makes it yummy! ? ?

"They're doing that to raise money for specific school activities," Principal Nichols says. "What are YOU raising money for?"

UH...THE NATE WRIGHT ALLOWANCE FUND? HA HA!...

HEH... HEH... ☆GULP!☆

ONLY $1.00

POOR NATE'S ALMANACK

Nothing. Not even a smile. Hey, remember that NICE principal who handed out juice boxes on the first day of school? Whatever happened to THAT guy?

"You may do business on your OWN time, Nate," he says sternly.

He walks off, probably looking for somebody else to boss around. This must be how Ben Franklin and the rest of the Founding Fathers felt about King George.

Teddy and I fold up the table and start down the hall. That's when things get crazy.

I hear Chad's voice from around the corner:

And then another voice:

Chad again:

I have no idea what's going on, but I hear footsteps coming our way. FAST footsteps.

We round the corner and finally I see what's happening. Randy just grabbed Chad's notebook. He's running this way. And he doesn't see us.

The table hits the floor. So does Randy. I see a flash of red on his face. Blood starts pouring from his nose.

This is awesome.

Randy doesn't hesitate. He looks right at Ms. Clarke, points at me . . . and lies through his teeth.

WHAT??? I open my mouth to protest, but Ms. Clarke speaks first.

THAT'S NOT WHAT **I** SAW.

"It looked to ME," she says, "like you gave yourSELF a bloody nose because you were running in the hall."

NATE WAS JUST MOVING A TABLE.

Randy looks stunned. Repeat: This . . . is . . . AWESOME!

Randy hesitates. Finally he turns to go. He glares at me as he brushes by, muttering something under his breath.

"What'd he say?" Teddy asks.

"I'm not sure," I answer. "Something about . . ."

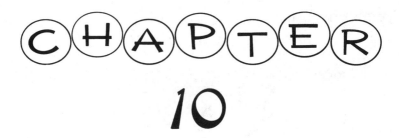

CHAPTER 10

Tomorrow's here already.

Bring it on. A winner-take-all game for the Spoffy?

"Oh, we're prepared, all right," I answer confidently.

There's a pause. Dad's looking at me like I've got
two heads.

"Fleeceball, obviously. What are YOU talking
about?"

He raises an eyebrow. "Your big social studies
project . . . OBVIOUSLY."

That's weird. Dad's usually
clueless about what's going on
at school. Now he wants to be Joe Details?

I don't really want him finding out about the
deal I made with Gina. So . . .

The guys rank on me all the way to school. But I can deal with it. Things are looking pretty good right now. Not only am I basically guaranteed an A plus for being Gina's project partner, I've pulled it off without having to do any actual WORK with her. How sweet is that?

We walk into Mrs. Godfrey's room, and suddenly it's a tension convention. Everybody's looking over their projects one last time, making sure they haven't forgotten anything. Which reminds me . . .

"What for?" she says.

Duh. Because I don't trust you, of course. It would be just like you to take my name off that thing at the last second.

"How come you put YOUR name first?" I ask.

"Are you SERIOUS?" she says fiercely.

Gina snatches it back from me. "I'LL give it to her," she growls, and makes a beeline for Mrs. Godfrey.

Gag me. Look at the way they're smiling at each other. Is this social studies or a family reunion? Just hand the stinkin' thing in, Gina.

Mrs. Godfrey starts flipping through it. Her smile slowly fades. What's THAT all about?

OH, DEAR...

"Oh, dear"? Did she say "oh, dear"?

"Is—is something wrong?" Gina says. Her voice sounds a tiny bit higher than usual.

"Can you tell me about these visual aids?" Mrs. Godfrey asks.

I glance at Gina. She looks . . . well, sort of . . . PANICKY.

I... UM... I PRINTED SOME OF THEM OFF THE INTERNET... AND I PHOTOCOPIED THE OTHERS FROM LIBRARY BOOKS...

Mrs. Godfrey frowns. "The instructions were very clear on this matter."

Visual aids are an important part of your project. You must create them yourself. Using or borrowing images from outside sources could result in a failing grade.

Gina's eyes open wide. So do mine. Her Royal Highness forgot to read the instructions? REALLY? Hey, anybody got a camera? I want to get a picture of this.

Her whole body starts to shake.

F-FAILING GRADE?

Wow. WOW! Could it be? Could Little Miss Perfect actually get an F?

"These projects are supposed to be one hundred percent original student work," Mrs. Godfrey says sternly.

Gina looks totally destroyed. What a moment. I'm going to enjoy this. I might never get this chance again.

"And, Nate . . . ," Mrs. Godfrey says, turning to me.

Gulp. Reality check. For a minute I forgot that
Gina and I are a TEAM for this stupid thing.

"Well, the two of you are PARTNERS, aren't you?"
she says impatiently.

Great. Thanks a LOT, Gina. I TOLD you we should
have used my . . .

I grab my Ben Franklin folder from my desk. Maybe . . . MAYBE! . . . this will undo Gina's screwup.

I can tell she's a little surprised,. but she opens the folder. Gina scooches over to me.

"What are you DOING?" she whispers angrily.

". . . Because in case you haven't noticed, Gina, YOUR brilliant visual aids just earned us an F!"

Gina and I wait as Mrs. Godfrey slowly looks at each page. She's not just skimming through it. She's actually READING the stuff. Hey, that works for me. There's some quality material there. Like my latest comic:

"Nate," Mrs. Godfrey says finally. "Did YOU draw all these cartoons?" She's not saying it in her usual crabby way. She actually looks HAPPY.

"Uh-huh," I say.

"These really ARE original, in the very best sense of the word," she continues. "They make this a one-of-a-kind project!"

Gina's losing it. Her face is all purple and she can barely talk. Is this what a heart attack looks like?

"Well, that's entirely appropriate for a Ben Franklin project," Mrs. Godfrey says. "Nate, I'm sure you can tell us why!"

For half a second I don't know what she's getting at. Then it hits me.

"He sometimes drew political cartoons and published them in his own newspaper," she explains. "And, Nate," she continues . . .

"Hear that, Gina?" I say.

Of course Gina can't help herself. "Can we still get an A plus on the project?" she blurts out.

Mrs. Godfrey waves us back to our desks. "No promises!" she says cheerily.

We sit down. Gina's not saying anything. Hey, fine with me. I've got PLENTY to say.

"Well, Gina, despite your bonehead mistake, it sounds like you'll get your precious A plus after all," I tell her.

She turns bright red. "It wasn't all YOU!" she hisses at me. "We BOTH contributed!"

"Right, right, whatever you say. Oh, and, Gina, there's just one more thing . . ."

She looks like her face might burst into flames. I can tell she wants to scream at me, but she can't say a thing. She knows I'm right. She knows that without me, her perfect academic record would have gone straight down the toilet.

Who knew getting an A plus could be so much fun?

11

You know what I hate? Waiting.

It's bad enough waiting around for everyday stuff, like the bathroom.

But when you're waiting for something really important, like our championship game against the Raptors? That's brutal. Everything moves in super slow motion.

It's only when the bell rings—FINALLY!—that time starts moving again. I fly out of the science lab, ditch my notebook, and head straight for the gym.

Randy's sort of hard to understand with his nose wrapped up like a pound of ground beef, so I'll translate. He just told me it's payback time. Guess he thinks he's got the better team.

There she is, talking to Coach. I've got to hand it to her: She promised not to play, and she hasn't. She invents a different excuse for every game.

Hm. Food poisoning. That's a new one. And today's lunch was so disgusting, it's 100 percent believable. Nice job, Gina.

But enough about her. We've got a game to win. There's only one problem:

Randy slams my very first pitch way up on the back wall. If a ball hits below the "Home of the Bobcats" banner, it's a double. If it hits above the banner, it's a home run.

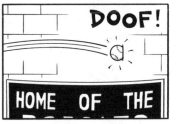

Randy showboats around the bases, a huge grin on his face. When he reaches home, he jumps on the plate like he just landed on the moon or something. What a jerk.

Here's the good thing about fleeceball, though: There's a lot of scoring. Falling behind 1–0 isn't the end of the world, because you'll probably catch up. And we do. After one inning, it's 2–1, Kuddle Kittens.

> If both teams continue to score at this rate, we'll win 18 to 9! Actually, make that **16** to 9, because, as the home team, we wouldn't bat in the bottom of the ninth because we blah blah blah blah blah blah blah blah...

Then it's 4–2, Raptors. Then 5–4, Kuddle Kittens. And then 6–5, Raptors. You get the idea. It's back and forth the whole game.

We reach the ninth inning tied, 9–9. And look who's up.

I hate to admit it, but Randy's a tough out. He's already gotten three hits today.

He always hits the ball hard. So it catches me a little by surprise . . .

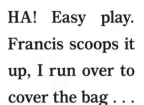

. . . when he dribbles a soft ground ball toward Francis at first base.

HA! Easy play. Francis scoops it up, I run over to cover the bag . . .

. . . and then it happens. Payback time.

It feels like my foot just exploded. Randy and I both hit the floor. He gets up right away, but I don't. I'm too busy rolling around in total agony.

What?? "These things happen"? Uh, yeah . . . whenever RANDY'S around. I thought Coach was smarter than that. Can't he see that Randy went for my foot on PURPOSE?

Francis and Teddy help me over to the bleachers, and Coach brings me an ice pack. "No more fleece-ball for you today, Nate," he says.

"Not necessarily!" chirps Chad.

What?? Chad, are you INSANE? "NO!" I shout immediately.

Coach gives me a funny look, then turns to Gina. "Your team could use your help, Gina. Are you well enough to play?"

She stares straight at me.

"Fantastic!" says Coach.

Apparently Coach doesn't realize how UNfantastic this is. In fact, this could be a complete disaster.

"Nothing." She smirks. "Just filling in for an injured teammate."

Oh, that's a riot. "Listen, Gina . . ."

Is she serious? "Dream ON, Gina." I snort.

Before she can bite my head off, Coach interrupts. "Enough talk, you two," he says. "Let's play ball."

As Gina walks out to right field, I can hear some of the Raptors laughing. I'm starting to get a really bad feeling about this.

At first, things go okay. The Raptors load the bases, but we manage to get two outs. All we need is one more to keep the score tied.

They hit it to Gina.

11–9, Raptors. We get the third out on the next pitch, but the damage is done. Thanks, Gina.

We still have one more chance to bat. The good news is: Teddy and Francis reach base with two outs. The bad news is: Here comes out number three.

Earth to Chad: No, she can't.

See? Her stuffed cat would have a better chance of getting a hit. This is awful. I can't just sit here and watch us lose. I've got to DO something!

She's speechless. But Coach isn't.

"SIT DOWN, Nate," he barks.

He means it. I let go of the broom handle and hobble back to the bleachers. This stinks. I'm the captain of the team, but I'm stuck watching.

Here it comes: the final pitch of the game.

For a few seconds the gym is completely silent. Then . . .

"HOME RUN!" screams Chad.

I don't say anything. I'm in shock. It's not until Coach walks toward us with the Spoffy that I actually believe my eyes.

"Congratulations, Kuddle Kittens!" he says. Then he hands the trophy to . . .

What's up with THAT? She plays ONE INNING and all of a sudden she's Joe All-Star?

Oop. Hold it, she's walking over here. Maybe she realizes that the TEAM CAPTAIN should get the Spoffy. Let's hear what she's got to say for herself.

Ouch. That was cold. She struts off, holding up the Spoffy like she's the Statue of Liberty. "What an amazing game!" I hear Chad tell her.

CHAPTER 12

Poor Nate's SPORTS WRAP

KUDDLE KITTENS WIN SPOFFY

Led by team captain *NATE WRIGHT*, the Kuddle Kittens (**real** name: Psycho Dogs) beat Randy Betancourt's Raptors in yesterday's fleeceball champion- ship, 12-11. A lucky hit in the ninth inning enabled the Kuddle Kittens to come back from a 2-run deficit

"LUCKY HIT?"

I spin around. Gina's reading over my shoulder. Can't a literary genius write in peace?

"You just hate that I saved us from losing!" she snarls.

"Oh, really?" I ask her.

"That was DIFFERENT!" she says, her voice rising. "I did the REAL work!"

"My comics aren't stupid, Gina," I shoot back at her, "which you'd KNOW if you'd spent a little time STUDYING them!"

"Wha . . . ? STUDYING?" she sputters. "Who are YOU to lecture ME about STUDYING?"

"Shouting is not permitted in the library, Gina," Mrs. Hickson says. She pulls out a little pink pad.

Gina gasps. "The—the detention room?"

"It's across the hall from the faculty lounge," I say helpfully.

She points at me, looking totally outraged. "YOU'RE the one who should go to detention!"

"Stop comparing yourself to Ben Franklin!" she hisses at me.

Oh, I don't know about that. Ben and I have a lot in common. I'll bet if he were alive today, he and I would get along pretty well.

I think he'd get a real charge out of me.

BIG NATE STARRING IN...

HOW TO DRAW ME!

HINT: SKETCH LIGHTLY AT FIRST, THEN MAKE LINES **BOLDER** TO FINISH YOUR DRAWING!

START WITH AN OVAL. SEE HOW IT'S WIDER AT THE TOP?

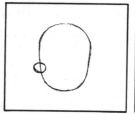

MAKE A SMALLER OVAL. THERE'S MY NOSE!

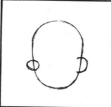

A LOOP (LIKE A BACKWARD "C") IS MY EAR.

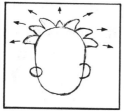

I HAVE SEVEN TUFTS OF HAIR. FOLLOW THE ARROWS!

MY EYES ARE EASY TO DRAW. THEY'RE TWO STRAIGHT LINES!

NOW ADD MY MOUTH SO I CAN SAY SOMETHING!

COLOR IN MY **HAIR**, ADD A NECK AND SHOULDERS, AND YOU'RE **DONE!**

GREAT JOB!

Lincoln Peirce

is a cartoonist/writer and the author of the *New York Times* bestsellers *Big Nate: In a Class by Himself*, *Big Nate Strikes Again*, and the collections *Big Nate: From the Top* and *Big Nate: Out Loud*, as well as *Big Nate Boredom Buster*. *Big Nate: In a Class by Himself* was selected for *Horn Book Magazine*'s Fanfare List of Best Books of 2010 and BarnesandNoble.com's Top Ten. Also, *Big Nate: In a Class by Himself* will be published in sixteen countries, including Turkey, Portugal, Germany, Brazil, Spain, France, Italy, Greece, Canada, China, Japan, Taiwan, Holland, the Czech Republic, Indonesia, and Israel, and will be translated into eighteen languages. Lincoln Peirce is also the creator of the comic strip *Big Nate*. It appears in two hundred and fifty U.S. newspapers and online daily at www.bignate.com.

Check out Big Nate Island at www.poptropica.com. And link to www.bignatebooks.com for games, blogs, and more information about the Big Nate series and the author, who lives with his wife and two children in Portland, Maine.